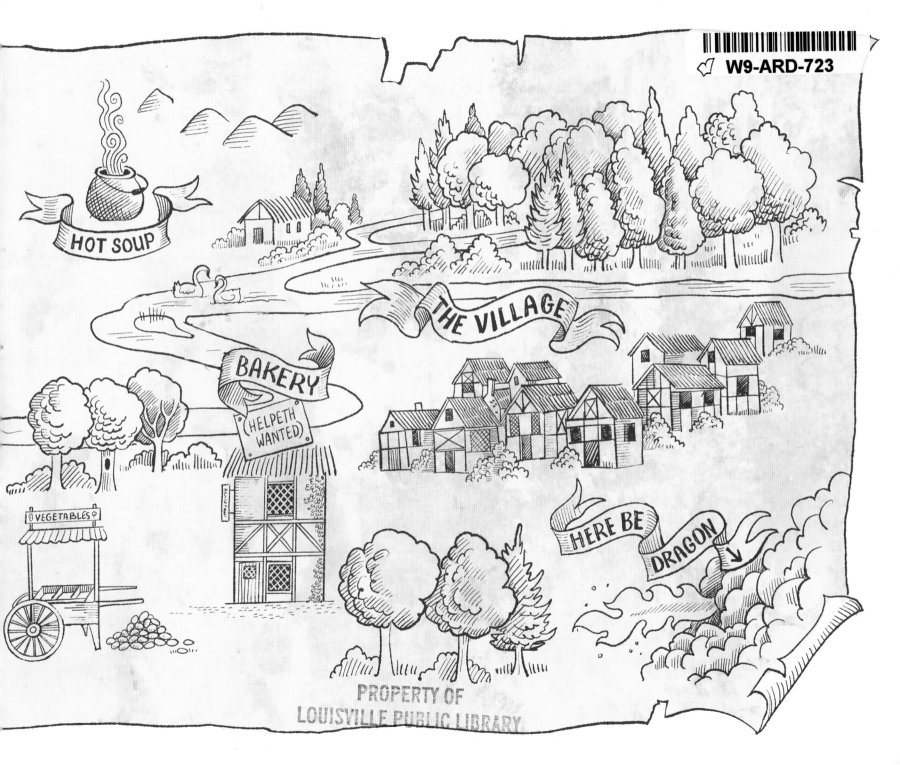

HOT SOUP

THE VILLAGE

BAKERY

(HELPETH WANTED)

VEGETABLES

HERE BE DRAGON

This is the story of the
Eight Knights of Hanukkah:
Sir Alex, Sir Gabriel, Sir Margaret,
Sir Julian, Sir Lily, Sir Henry,
Sir Isabella, and Sir Rugelach.
And that's the Eight Knights'
mother, Lady Sadie.

The Eight Knights

OF HANUKKAH

by Leslie Kimmelman

illustrated by Galia Bernstein

HOLIDAY HOUSE · NEW YORK

Lady Sadie called the Eight Knights of Hanukkah together. "Tonight is the last night of Hanukkah. I invited the entire kingdom to celebrate with us, but alas! A dastardly dragon named Dreadful is roaming the countryside, interrupting the party preparations. My children, I am counting on you to fix things with some deeds of awesome kindness and stupendous bravery."

"Challenge accepted," said the knights.

"I will tame the dragon," said Sir Isabella.

"Stupendous bravery is my specialty,"
added Sir Rugelach, his mouth full of cookie.

"Bye, Mommy," said Sir Henry.

Off the knights rode.

The first knight, Sir Alex, cantered into a village on his trusty steed.

"Hark!" he exclaimed. "Methinks I hear a crying child."

He jumped from the horse and crouched down beside the boy.

"What be the matter, young lad?" he asked.

"The dragon scorched my dreidel," the boy sniffed. "The only Hebrew letter left is *nun*, which means I always lose."

"I will make you a new dreidel,"
Sir Alex said, picking up a piece of wood.
He carved a *nun* first, then *gimmel*, *hey*,
and *shin* on the other sides.

"The letters stand for *Nes gadol hayah sham*.
Which means, 'A great miracle happened there.'"

The boy spun the dreidel.

"Thanks!" he shouted happily.

"*Gimmel* is the best letter of all!
It *is* a miracle."

Sir Alex waved as he sped off.
"Happy Hanukkah, young lad!
I shall see you tonight."

 eanwhile . . . Sir Isabella and Sir Rugelach searched high and low for Dreadful.

P a-da-thump! Pa-da-thump! The second knight, Sir Gabriel, galloped across the plains on his silver stallion.

"Hark!" he exclaimed. "Methinks I hear a damsel in distress."

A woman was wailing over an enormous pile of potatoes.

"Why do you weep, fair lady?" asked the knight.

"I must peel these potatoes to make Hanukkah latkes for the townsfolk tonight," she replied. "But alas and alack, the dragon has scared off my helpers."

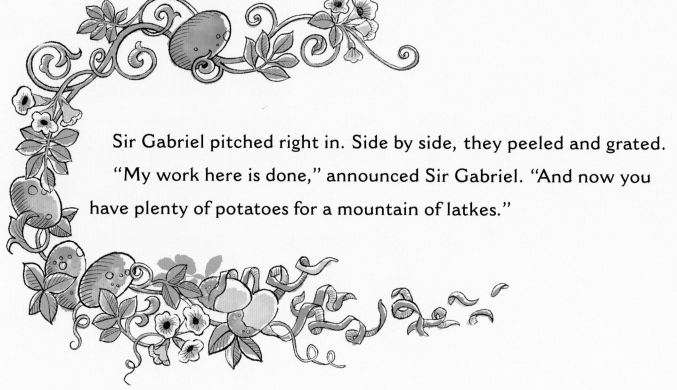

Sir Gabriel pitched right in. Side by side, they peeled and grated.

"My work here is done," announced Sir Gabriel. "And now you

have plenty of potatoes for a mountain of latkes."

Meanwhile . . .
Sir Isabella and
Sir Rugelach looked
north, south, east,
and west.

"Show your face, you fire-breathing bully!" shouted Sir Rugelach.

"Please," added Sir Isabella.

Still no dragon.

M-m-m-m. The third knight, Sir Margaret, made her way through a sweet-smelling fruit orchard.

"Hark! Methinks I see some sad-faced field hands," Sir Margaret exclaimed. "What ails you, fair people?"

"We need apples for applesauce for the Hanukkah latkes," answered a young maiden.

"But when we climb the tree to pick them," explained a young man, "the dragon flies low, and poof! Baked apples!"

"Fear not," Sir Margaret replied. "My long and noble lance can knock down the fruit you seek."

Many baskets of apples later,
Sir Margaret was on her way.
"My work here is done,"
she called back. "I will see
you when the sun goes down."

Meanwhile . . . Sir Isabella
and Sir Rugelach kept coming
after the dragon. They gave chase—
and got chased—dodging smoke and fire.

Sir Julian, the fourth knight, performed the mitzvah of bringing chicken soup to the sick and keeping company with the lonely.

The soup was delicious. The talk was lively. The jokes were funny.

Everyone felt better right away, because laughter is the best medicine.

"Just in time for the party," they agreed happily.

HELPETH WANTED read the sign Sir Lily, the fifth knight, saw in a bakery window.

"We made dozens of Hanukkah donuts for the celebration," complained the chief baker. "Then Dreadful swooped down and gobbled every one."

"Worryeth not," said Sir Lily.

She worked alongside the bakers all day long, making *sufganiyot*.
She braved a hot stove, sizzling oil, and sticky, drippy jam.

"Those things are nothing at all to a knight such as I," said
Sir Lily modestly.

The sixth knight, Sir Henry, rode out with the others. Then he turned his horse around and trotted back to the castle.

"Why do you not venture out to do deeds of awesome kindness and stupendous bravery?" asked Lady Sadie.

"I stay *in* and do acts of awesome kindness and stupendous bravery," answered Sir Henry.

The goodly Sir Henry cleaned the castle till it gleamed.

He swept the drawbridge and chased away two ferocious-looking lizards. Stupendous bravery.

He brought Lady Sadie
a cup of hot tea and a fluffy
pillow for her tired feet.
Awesome kindness.

Meanwhile . . . the seventh and eighth knights, Sir Isabella
and Sir Rugelach, were feeling discouraged. They just couldn't catch
that dragon. They sat, thinking, and the air got warmer and warmer.

Uh-oh! Dreadful!

"But you're just a *baby* dragon!" exclaimed Sir Isabella.

"And my name isn't Dreadful." The dragon sniffed. "It's Rosie."

So Rosie was invited to the Hanukkah celebration.

he sun sank in the sky. One by one, the knights returned home. At their big Round Table, the Eight Knights of Hanukkah exchanged tales of spectacular deeds and derring-do.

Before long, guests began to arrive.

Never had the Round Table been graced by so many heroic knights, nor the castle grounds with so much merrymaking.

HOOSH! Rosie lit the Hanukkah candles.

It was a most excellent Hanukkah. The Eight Knights of Hanukkah had lit up the darkness of the world with the bright light of kindness.

Shine on, good knights, shine on!

The Traditions of Hanukkah

Over two thousand years ago in ancient Judea (roughly modern-day Israel), a group of Jews led by Judah Maccabee and his brothers fought King Antiochus of Syria for the right to practice their religion. The holiday of Hanukkah celebrates the Maccabees' victory.

It also celebrates the miracle that followed the victory: Inside the temple, one day's lamp oil burned for eight days and nights. Today we remember these miracles by lighting candles in the menorah for eight nights, and by eating latkes and sufganiyot that have been fried in oil. When the dreidel is spun round, the letters on its sides remind us, "A great miracle happened there."

At Hanukkah, and all year round, doing mitzvoth—good deeds—is an important part of Judaism.

Methinks you can find some deeds of awesome kindness to do in your own kingdom!

To Kama, who performs deeds of awesome kindness
all the time.—L.K.

To Sir Dafna, who stayed in,
and did acts of stupendous bravery.—G.B.

Library of Congress Cataloging-in-Publication Data

Names: Kimmelman, Leslie, author. | Bernstein, Galia, illustrator.
Title: The Eight Knights of Hanukkah / by Leslie Kimmelman ; illustrated by Galia Bernstein.
Description: First edition. | New York : Holiday House, [2020] | Summary: On the last night
of Hanukkah, Lady Sadie summons her children, the Eight Knights of Hanukkah, to stop the
dastardly dragon that is interrupting party preparations, using kindness and bravery. Includes notes
on the traditions of Hanukkah and directions for playing the dreidel game.
Identifiers: LCCN 2019012557 | ISBN 9780823439584 (hardcover)
Subjects: | CYAC: Knights and knighthood—Fiction. | Dragons—Fiction.
Behavior—Fiction. | Hanukkah—Fiction. | Jews—Fiction.
Classification: LCC PZ7.K56493 Eig 2020 | DDC [E]—dc23
LC record available at https://lccn.loc.gov/2019012557

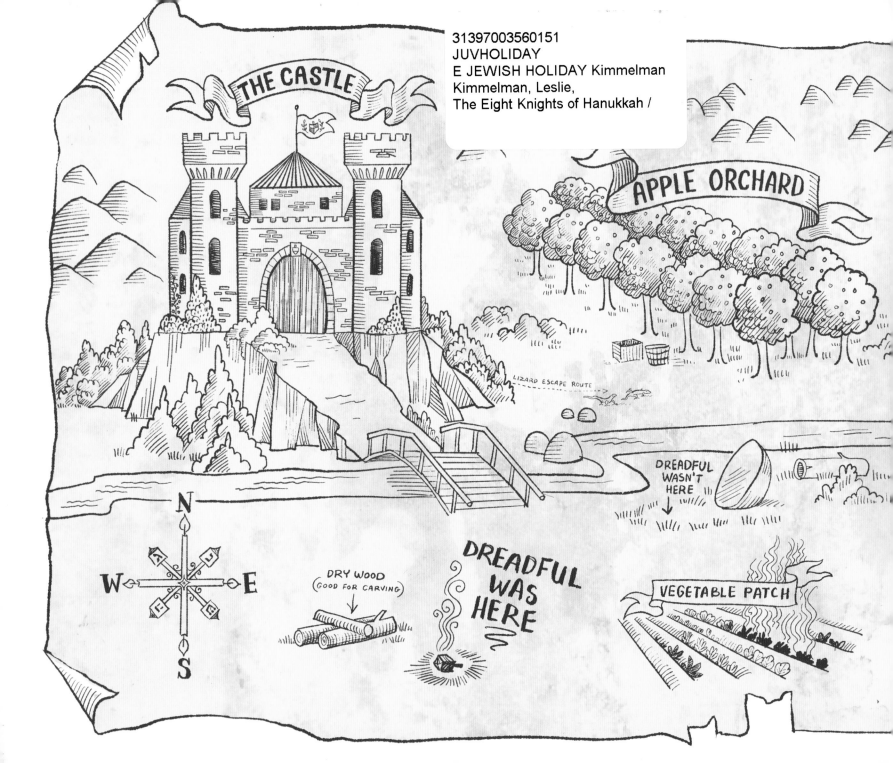